WIZARDS, WARRIORS & YOU
is a game of fantasy role-playing as well as a book.

In each adventure, you will choose to play the game as either the Wizard or the Warrior. Wearing the Wizard's robes, you will summon up magical spells to fend off your enemies. Carrying the Warrior's sword, you will use your strength and brilliance in battle to prevail against all challengers.

There are dozens of adventures in this book. If you choose to play the role of the Wizard, all of the mysterious spells in *The Book of Spells* at the back of this book will be at your command. Use them to guide the Wizard past peril after peril.

Then close the book and start all over again, this time as the Warrior. Try your skill with all of the weapons listed in *The Book of Weapons*, also found at the back of this book.

No matter which role you choose to play, you will face new challenges, battle surprising foes, and make life-or-death decisions on every page!

Other Avon Books in the
WIZARDS, WARRIORS & YOU™ SERIES

BOOK 1: The Forest of Twisted Dreams
by R. L. Stine

Available November 1984
BOOK 3: Who Kidnapped Princess Saralinda?
by Megan Stine & H. William Stine

BOOK 4: Ghost Knights of Camelot
by David Anthony Kraft

WIZARDS, WARRIORS & YOU™

BOOK 2

The Siege of the Dragonriders

by Eric Affabee
illustrated by Earl Norem
A Parachute Press Book

AVON
PUBLISHERS OF BARD, CAMELOT, DISCUS AND FLARE BOOKS

WIZARDS, WARRIORS & YOU™: THE SIEGE OF THE
DRAGONRIDERS is an original publication of Avon Books.
This work has never before appeared in book form.

AVON BOOKS
A divison of
The Hearst Corporation
1790 Broadway
New York, New York 10019

Introduction

Past the pale stone castle, where King Henry rules, past the green courtyard where Henry's knights train and meet in the competition of the joust, past the meadows where the King's cows graze, past the vineyards where the King's wine is pressed, past the marketplace, past the village inns, past the farms, several hundred yards beyond the low brick wall that forms the very boundary of the royal domain, stands a large, flat rock.

This large, flat rock is bounded by a steep, jagged cliff on one side and the rolling purple ocean on the other. It is on this flat rock that the Wizard and the Warrior meet to remember adventures of the past and to talk of adventures yet to come.

They have much to talk about.

Together, this team of legend—this master of magical forces and this champion of the lightning sword—have defeated evil in this world and in worlds beyond. They have triumphed over untold foes in castles and courtyards, and in the mountains and forests that surround the medieval world.

The challenges of this world are many. For there are always those—human and nonhuman—who would destroy the Wizard and the Warrior and the world they protect.

In this book, you will enter the unpredictable world of the Wizard and the Warrior. You will enter the world—and you will become part of it.

If you make the right decisions, the Wizard and the Warrior will succeed in their quest, and their legend will live on. If you make the wrong choices, their bright legend will dim, and you will find yourself trapped in a world of unimagined horrors.

The journey into the world of *WIZARDS, WARRIORS AND YOU* begins on PAGE 1.

Let it be known that the amazing tale of all that came to pass for the Wizard and the Warrior in their battle against the dragonriders is true. The adventure began on a cloudy autumn day in the tenth year of the reign of King Henry, in the meadow outside the walls of Silvergate, his castle.

The wind blew cool across the tall grass of the meadow as the Wizard and the Warrior stepped forward to join the rest of King Henry's subjects. It was the day before the harvest, a day of solemn prayers followed by celebration.

As the chanting of the priest floated on the wind, a cloud spread its darkness over the sun, and a chill covered the crowded meadow. "A rain today would surely slow the harvest," the Wizard said quietly to his companion, his eyes surveying the sky.

"But we have much to be thankful for," the Warrior answered, ignoring the cold wind that blew against his ceremonial armor. "The crops are plentiful this year. No one will go hungry."

The Wizard looked toward the large barrels of wine, carried to the meadow for the daylong celebration that would follow the priest's blessings. "And I believe that no one will go thirsty, either," he said, a smile crossing his usually serious face.

The priest finished his melodious prayers and stepped back. King Henry stepped forward to speak his official pronouncement of the harvest. He raised his hands as greeting to his subjects.

But he didn't get to say a word.

The dark clouds suddenly turned darker, and the wind picked up. The clouds seemed to swirl about, gray upon gray, black upon gray, twisting, undulating faster and faster.

All eyes were on the sky now. What storm was this that threatened to interrupt the celebration?

"Look! Someone rides the clouds!" a farmer yelled, his arm tightening around the shoulder of his frightened wife.

Figures appeared in the swirling, twisting clouds—giant figures that resembled men, then monsters, then men astride monsters!

"What monsters are these!" the Warrior cried, reaching for the Sword of the Golden Lion, which was always at his side.

Closer the giant figures loomed, shadows against the shadowy clouds. The sky rumbled. The rumble became a roar that shook the meadowland.

"Dragons!" several terrified people screamed at once.

The sky above the kingdom was darkened now, not by clouds but by an army of gigantic, winged dragons. And on each flying beast rode a warrior in black armor, carrying a spear of black.

"Warriors who ride atop dragons!" the Wizard cried. "Is this magic? Has some evil sorcerer bewitched my eyes?"

His question was answered quickly. The dragons

and their fierce riders were real. The dragons landed in the farmland that stretched beyond the meadow and roared a menacing greeting.

As King Henry and his subjects watched in horror and fright, the giant beasts trampled the ripe crops. Urged on by the warriors who rode them as if they were horses, they smashed and burned the wheat, the barley, and the vegetables that had been grown with such care—all were flattened beneath their deliberate footsteps and then turned to ash by their fiery breath.

The King's warriors stood frozen in amazement as this army of monsters and men destroyed all of the crops of the North lands. "We shall return!" a warrior's voice called from atop a heaving, hissing dragon. "This kingdom—and all kingdoms—shall be ours!"

The dragonriders turned their beasts, two hundred beasts at least, treading once again over the crops they had already destroyed. Slowly, arrogantly, keeping to the ground—daring the King's men to follow—they rode off toward the forests beyond the farmlands.

King Henry's grief-stricken subjects returned in silence to their homes, thinking of the long, hungry winter they soon were to face. The meadow stood empty, the wine barrels lying alone, unattended under the dark sky.

Soon after, the Wizard and the Warrior were summoned to the King's chamber. "Men who can tame winged dragons and ride them to battle!" the King exclaimed sadly, shaking his head. "I have never seen or heard such a thing in all my journeys!"

"If the dragons can be tamed by men, they can be tamed by *us!*" the Warrior said firmly. "Once the dragons have been defeated, the dragonriders can be beaten as well." The Wizard nodded agreement.

"I must rely on you," the King said. "If the crops of the South lands are also destroyed, none of us will survive the winter. You must follow these dragonriders. You must learn their secrets and in learning their secrets, discover a way to destroy them. This must be done before they can attack again."

"Excellency," said the Warrior, "we will not fail you."

Thus the tale begins. The story now becomes *your* story, the mission becomes *your* mission. The time has come for you to choose the role you wish to play.

Will you take the part of the WIZARD or the WARRIOR? Make your choice.

If you choose to be the Wizard, turn to PAGE 15.

If you choose to be the Warrior, turn to PAGE 17.

You draw your cloak around you and begin to chant the familiar words of Move Time Back. The sky turns red, then yellow. The animals of the forest fall silent. All that can be heard are your quiet words of magic.

FLASH!

You open your eyes. Down from the sky, the army of dragonriders is descending.

Your spell has worked. You have moved time back to the moment of the dragonriders' flight.

The dragons land, roaring in fury.

"We must climb onto one of the dragons!" the Warrior cries. "But how can we get near enough?"

"I will attempt the Momentary Darkness spell," you say, recalling Spell #3. "It should give us time enough to run across the field and sneak up behind one of them."

"And if the spell fails?" he asks.

"We've had a short but interesting life," you reply.

Smiling, you draw your dark cloak around you and prepare once again to summon the forces of magic to do your bidding.

Will you be able to create Momentary Darkness?

Toss two coins.

If they come up the same (two heads, two tails), turn to PAGE 91.

If they come up different, turn to PAGE 57.

You recite the words of the spell, summoning the force of your magic to combat the magic that has been left behind by the dragonriders. This spell takes all of your concentration, all of your energies—and if it doesn't succeed, your journey will be over before it has begun.

Will your spell succeed? A powerful spell like Combat Magic is always unpredictable. There is always the element of chance.

Flip a coin three times.

If you get at least two heads, turn to PAGE 48.

If you don't get at least two heads, turn to PAGE 16.

You do not sleep well the night before you and the Wizard are to begin your mission. You pace the floor of your chamber, your mind unable to cast away the picture of the dragonriders and their cruel attack.

Morning finally arrives, damp and cold. You and the Wizard mount your horses in silence. The harvest of the South lands has begun. As you and your companion ride by the fields, farmers drop their scythes to greet you and wish you well. Their words of hope are a sharp contrast to their frightened faces.

When you reach the gate that leads out of the kingdom, the Wizard finally breaks the silence. "I will never forget the sight of those monstrous creatures dropping down onto our land from the skies," he says sadly.

"It is possible that that is only the beginning of the horrors we will witness," you say grimly. Your horse edges back toward the gate, reluctant to leave the safety of the kingdom.

You realize that you must now come up with a strategy.

"At least the trail will not be hard to follow," the Wizard says, pointing to the wide path of destruction, the deep ruts in the earth, the singed grasslands left by the departing dragons.

"I am not so certain we wish to follow the path they have made," you say thoughtfully.

"But we have no other path to follow," the Wizard says. "No other guide."

"There is one other," you say. "There is Jebbarra."

Go on to PAGE 9.

The Wizard pulls his horse up short and turns to you with a wild look in his eyes. "Has the sight of those dragonriders dislodged your mind? Why would anyone seek out Jebbarra who has no cause to? Jebbarra is a dragon like those who attacked us, an aged dragon but still deadly."

"This path may end before leading us to the dragonriders' kingdom," you argue. "It is likely that the dragons took to the sky. They will have left no path for us to follow in the sky!"

"But to seek out Jebbarra in his cave is to—"

"Jebbarra is the only creature who can tell us from where these dragons and their masters come," you interrupt. "Jebbarra deals with the world of evil."

"Jebbarra *is* evil!" the Wizard cries. "And his evil is old enough to challenge my magic with success."

"But Jebbarra is old and tired," you insist. "He will not wish to rouse himself to challenge my sword."

"It is an unnecessary risk to take," the Wizard says. "I beg you to follow this path. Surely it will lead us to our enemy."

You must decide. Do you choose to pay a visit to Jebbarra, the ancient dragon, or to follow the trail the dragonriders have left?

If you choose to face Jebbarra, turn to PAGE 26.

If you choose to follow the trail, turn to PAGE 32.

FLASH!

From a distance you hear the thunder of a powerful wind. Closer, closer it comes. It blows past you. It seems to leap above you.

The dragon rears up as the wind attacks him. Zollah is lifted from his feet by the powerful wind. His face shows outrage!

You watch as the dragonriders take to the air and flee. You cannot catch them — but perhaps this time when you cast the spell to reverse time, the timing will be right. And you will be able to catch the dragonriders and ride with them to their true leader.

However, if the Move Time Back spell fails this time, you will not have the strength for more magic. And your mission will fail!

Flip a coin and hope that your magic will be strong.

If the coin comes up heads, turn to PAGE 6.
If the coin comes up tails, turn to PAGE 64.

The dragon keeps circling you. The circle becomes smaller each time it goes around.

"We will not fight!" the Warrior cries. "Take us to your masters."

The dragon gets a quizzical look on its scaly face. Perhaps it is not a talking dragon.

"Take us to those who ride on dragons! We will go willingly!" the Warrior cries.

The dragon seems to chuckle.

"I do not know of such things," the dragon says, his voice a harsh whisper from deep in his throat. "I do not know of masters or men who ride dragons. I only know that it is my lunchtime."

The dragon attacks his lunch swiftly, hungrily.

If this episode leaves *you* hungry for a happier ending, close the book and try again.

END

The sun is high in the sky as you reach the hill. It grows warm inside your armor. But you do not notice. You are thinking only of the challenge ahead, the challenge to find Jebbarra and persuade him to tell you what you want to know.

You decide to enter the first cave. A large serpent appears to drowse at the entrance.

"I will try a sleep spell," the Wizard says. "If the serpent truly sleeps, we can enter the cave easily." The Wizard draws his robes around him and begins to chant the words of the spell.

Suddenly he stops. "Jebbarra's magic seems stronger than mine," he says, shaken. "My words are driven back at me almost before I can say them."

"Jebbarra has magic to match his years," you say quietly. "My sword will gain us entry to this cave." You both climb off your horses and walk slowly up the hill to the cave entrance. The serpent at the opening is as tall as a man.

You draw the Sword of the Golden Lion from its scabbard and prepare to challenge the venomous guard.

The serpent sees you approaching. It lifts its head, pulls it back into attack position. Then it lifts another head . . . and another head!

To your amazement, you are about to do battle with a three-headed serpent!

Go on to PAGE 13.

All three heads begin to hiss as you steadily make your approach. The sound is deafening, but you move forward fearlessly, your eyes trying to follow all three heads.

You raise your sword. Your arm is ready to attack. You know you must chop off all three heads to defeat the serpent and gain entrance to the cave. Even if the snake is left with only one head, it will survive — and conquer!

Can you defeat this three-headed foe?

Flip a coin seven times. You must get *three heads* out of the seven throws.

If the coin comes up heads at least three times out of your seven throws, you have defeated the serpent. You and the Wizard can proceed through Cave No. 1 into Cave No. 2. Turn to PAGE 36.

If you do not come up with three heads out of seven throws, the serpent has defeated you. Your quest ends here at the mouth of this dark cave.

Unless you reopen this book and start another adventure . . .

The dragon heads move in for their dinner. You reach for one of your bows. You have only a few seconds to kill all four bodies. Perhaps your skill as an archer — and a little luck — will lead you to victory against this foe.

Using either the triple crossbow or the longbow with poison-tipped arrows, you have only a 50 percent chance of victory. Pick a number between one and ten.

If you picked 3, 4, 5, 6, or 7, your luck has run out. The hungry beast has ignored your arrows and is about to enjoy a tasty dinner of Wizard and Warrior. Close the book quickly before you are forced to read a more colorful description of what is about to happen to you.

If you picked 1, 2, 8, 9, or 10, your aim is true and your powerful weapon effective. All four heads cry out at once, and the dragon falls to the ground, four bodies toppling over as one.

You have won! But your victory is not entirely sweet. Turn to PAGE 66.

Instructions for the Wizard:

You have chosen the role of the Wizard. To combat the mysterious dragons and the warriors who have tamed them will require your most astonishing and powerful magical spells. In all of your years as a wizard, you have not faced foes as gigantic, as menacing as these.

At the back of this book (on page 97) you will find a book explaining all the magical spells your wizardry has taught you to perform. Turn now to *The Book of Spells*. Read them over quickly to get an idea of the powers you possess.

Turn to PAGE 20 to begin your quest to defeat the evil dragonriders.

FLASH!

The trees shake. Clouds fall from the sky.

Your spell has worked! The shield has been removed.

You slump to the forest floor, breathing heavily, feeling weak, every muscle in your body aching. "We — we must rest now," you manage to say to your companion.

The Warrior, too, is dazed from the force of your magic.

He is so dazed that he doesn't even see the pack of dragonwolves that are running to attack you now that the invisible wall is no longer there.

"Dragonwolves!" you call out weakly. "They must have been left as further protection by — by — "

It is too late. The beasts are already upon the Warrior. You are too weak to cast a spell to battle them. You are about to become their next meal.

Quick. Escape this tasteless scene. Close the book. Then try another adventure as you try to put a happier end to the siege of the dragonriders.

END

Instructions for the Warrior:

You are the Warrior. You have wisdom as well as might, so you realize that your boasts to the King were mere words. To defeat a huge army of winged dragons and the warriors who have tamed them will require more than words. It will require all of your skills as the Warrior.

At the back of this book, on page 101, you will find a book describing all the weapons you possess. Turn now to *The Book of Weapons*. You may take *only three* of these weapons along with you, in addition to the Sword of the Golden Lion, which is always with you. Choose carefully. Decide which three weapons you will take.

Turn to PAGE 8 to begin your hunt for the evil dragonriders.

The third cave appears to be empty as you approach, but you draw your sword, your hand tightening around the hilt, ready for whatever secrets the cave might hold. Your eyes dart back and forth quickly. All your powers, all your thoughts are concentrated on what might await you in the ancient dragon's den.

Into the darkness you and your companion walk, leading your horses as far into the cavern as you can. When the ceiling dips and the passageway grows narrow, you are forced to tether them. Their low whinnying echos loudly off the cave walls. It's the only sound you hear as you walk deeper, deeper into the darkness.

The pathway through the empty cavern becomes damp and muddy. You find yourself climbing a steep hill, then descending. You wander in silence for an hour, then another hour.

Finally you stop to rest. "Perhaps this pathway leads nowhere," you say to the Wizard. "Perhaps we will walk in this dank cave forever without ever seeing the light of day again. Dragons have been known to build such tortuous traps."

"What has a beginning must have an end," the Wizard says thoughtfully. "We have no choice but to proceed. We must find Jebbarra, or our mission is doomed before it has begun."

Go on to PAGE 19.

Walking slowly, you begin again to follow the twisting, climbing passageway through the dark cavern. After a few more hours, the ground becomes flat and sandy. The air feels dry. A soft breeze blows from up ahead. The darkness is broken by a dim, gray light.

"We must be near another opening," you say, picking up your pace, hurrying toward the light.

But you find no opening. Instead you find a fork in the path. One path leads up into more darkness. A second path curves into the light and disappears in the grayness.

"It seems we must make a choice," the Wizard says.

Which path do you believe will take you to Jebbarra? Do you choose the path into darkness, or the path into light?

If you choose the path into darkness, turn to PAGE 25.

If you choose the path into light, turn to PAGE 35.

The morning dawns gray and damp. You and the Warrior climb up onto stiff, cold saddles. Your horses shiver beneath you, still cold from their sleep.

You and your companion direct your horses toward the trail of destruction left by the dragons and their riders. You pass through the South lands, where the harvest has already begun. The farmers stop to cheer you as you pass by. "Will they really have something to cheer about?" you ask the Warrior hesitantly. "Or will the dragonriders return to destroy the remaining crops?"

"That I can only answer with my hopes," the Warrior replies somberly. "For at the end of this trail lies a mystery."

At sunset, you soon reach the edge of Silver Forest. You stop and look at the broken trees, the gaping ruts and holes in the forest ground, the burned shrubs and wild flowers. "I will use all of my magical knowledge to destroy these men who use dragons for evil," you say, nearly moved to tears by the scene of destruction.

"My weapons stand ready to back up your magic," the Warrior says, urging his horse forward into the forest darkness.

Go on to PAGE 21.

But his horse will not go forward.

It hits some sort of invisible barrier and falls backward, knocking the Warrior to the ground. "What sort of magic is this?" he cries, instinctively drawing his sword.

You climb down off your horse and walk forward slowly with your arms extended in front of you. After a few steps, you can feel the invisible wall that holds you back from entering the forest.

"They seem to have left a small obstacle in our path," you say. "The Invisible Shield is a rather crude spell, but good enough to keep us from following the trail."

"What can we do?" the Warrior asks. He slashes at the invisible wall with his sword, but it does not penetrate the barrier.

"I will try the Combat Magic spell," you tell him. "It is a powerful spell and requires so much of my energy that I will be able to use no *magic* for an entire day!"

"We have no choice," says the Warrior grimly. "We are completely encircled by this magical wall."

You draw your robes around you tightly and begin to chant the words to this powerful spell. Will you succeed? Can you remove the invisible wall that holds you prisoner?

Turn to PAGE 7.

As the dragon that you and the Warrior ride descends, you realize this must be the home of the dragonriders. The roar of the multitude of dragons below is nearly deafening. Down, down the dragon swoops, down to the head of the clearing, down so fast you close your eyes to protect them from the wind.

But there is no way to protect your ears from the roar of the dragons on the ground, the cheers of the dragonriders, the din of clanging armor, pounding dragons' feet, cries of victory and delight as all in this evil army realize that you have been captured.

THUD. You hit the ground. The dragon beneath you seems to bounce. You grab at the scaly back to keep from falling off.

"What horror awaits us here?" the Warrior asks.

You do not have to wait long before the question is answered.

A familiar figure lumbers forward, a gigantic figure you have seen before, a figure you have wished never to see again.

"Zollah! It is you!!" you cry.

For indeed it is an old enemy of yours. It is the mighty dragon, Zollah — Zollah the Unimaginable!

Go on to PAGE 23.

"I bid you welcome," Zollah bellows, its powerful voice echoing through the trees. "Pity your stay will be a short one."

The dragons in the clearing roar their approval.

"I see you are marveling at my accomplishment here," Zollah exclaims, reaching a powerful arm over and grabbing you off the dragon that brought you to this astounding scene, holding you high in the air so that you may view the vast army. "It wasn't difficult to tame humans and teach them to ride my brethren!" Zollah cries.

"You mean — the men who ride the dragons — " you begin.

"Yes, they are all under my spell," Zollah says, grinning a toothy grin. "Did you think it the other way around? Did you think that men could tame dragons?" Zollah's laugh shakes the forest and is echoed by the thunderous laughter of two hundred dragons. "With the help of my human slaves, dragons will once again take their places as monarchs of all the kingdoms of earth!" Zollah cries.

As Zollah talks, your mind whirls. You realize you do not have much time to try to defeat this monstrous foe.

Turn to PAGE 63.

Warrick slumps over the railing of the balcony. "I feel weak . . . so weak . . ." he cries. Your magic has proved the stronger.

"I will finish him off!" the Warrior cries, grabbing his sword.

"No," you say, pulling back his arm. "I cannot allow it. Run, brother!" you yell up to your weakened adversary. "I will allow you to flee this place! I cannot kill my own brother!"

You watch as Warrick struggles to stand. He turns and without looking back runs into the castle. You know that he will flee. You do not need to follow him.

Meanwhile, the dragons have turned on their former masters. Warrick's spell over them broken, the dragons move forward to seek revenge against the men who dared treat them as beasts of burden. Soon the black rock of the castle courtyard is stained with dark red blood.

"Let us return home," you call to the Warrior. You pull him away from the scene of hideous slaughter. "The journey home is a long one."

"A victorious journey is always short," the Warrior says with a grin.

"The way home is always long when you are as heartsick as I!" you cry, as the two of you walk away from the black castle into the sunlight. Once again the Wizard and the Warrior have triumphed!

END

If you would like to play the role of the Warrior when you set out on your next adventure, turn to PAGE 17.

The path into darkness leads up, up until the air feels thin and you struggle for each breath. Still you climb, your sword ready, your whole body tensed and ready to battle any foe you may encounter.

You wander for hours, blindly following the path. Your footsteps drag against the dirt path. Your whole body aches from the miles you have walked — miles of uncertainty, dark miles of your desperate search.

"Look — up ahead! A dim light!" you cry.

"It appears to be the entrance to another cave.

The path into darkness has led you up to Cave No. 2.

Is this where the ancient Jebbarra resides?

To enter this cave, turn to PAGE 36.

Jebbarra, the ancient dragon, has not left his cave in more than a hundred years. The wise old creature lives in a hill of dark caves connected by even darker tunnels — a labyrinth of safety, for few have dared to enter these caves. Even fewer have come out again.

You are willing to risk a confrontation with the dragon because you are certain Jebbarra will be able to guide you to the dragonriders. But to confront Jebbarra, you must first find him.

As you approach the Hill of Jebbarra's Labyrinth, you see that there are four caves. You must guess which cave will lead you to Jebbarra.

At the entrance to Cave No. 1, you see what appears to be a large serpent acting as guard. Cave No. 2 appears to be empty — but, of course, you cannot know if it is truly empty without entering. Cave No. 3 also appears to be empty. Cave No. 4 seems to have some sort of white covering draped over the entranceway. Is this because Jebbarra is inside?

Which cave do you choose to enter?

If you choose Cave #1, turn to PAGE 12.
If you choose Cave #2, turn to PAGE 36.
If you choose Cave #3, turn to PAGE 18.
If you choose Cave #4, turn to PAGE 50.

A shudder runs down the ancient dragon's body. Jebbarra closes his eyes and shakes his head slowly. He stands still now, as still as death.

"I have entertained you, Jebbarra, have I not? I have entertained you, and I have killed your soldiers here!" you shout, pointing at the corpses of the spiderdragons.

Silence from the old dragon.

"Now you must give me the information I request," you cry, pointing the Sword of the Golden Lion up at the giant dragon.

Silence. Jebbarra appears to be in a trance. Or is it just sleep?

A fit of violent coughing arouses the dragon. One eye opens, then the other, and its face contorts into a hideous frown.

"You have invaded my home and committed murder," the raspy voice of Jebbarra cries out.

"I entered your home and was attacked," you argue, standing your ground. "I will not stay here any longer than I need to. Keep your bargain, old one. Keep your bargain, and tell my companion and me where we might find the foes we seek."

Go on to PAGE 29.

Jebbarra coughs, then slowly nods agreement.

"I live in two worlds," he tells you quietly. "Your world and the world of twilight evil. I will tell you two tales. One contains the information you seek. One is a tale not of your time or place. I cannot tell you which tale to believe. That you must decide for yourself."

"Tell us your tales, Jebbarra," you insist impatiently.

To hear Jebbarra's tales, turn to **PAGE 44**.

The two of you rest for a while, alone in this clearing where a few moments ago a large audience of men and dragons watched your battle against Zollah.

"Our victory was snatched away from us with the dragonriders' flight," the Warrior says quietly.

"Our victory was snatched away from us when Zollah chose to deceive us," you say.

"How shall we follow the dragonriders now?" the Warrior asks, shaking his head. "Our horses cannot follow a trail in the sky."

The two of you sit in silence.

Soon you have an idea. "I believe I can call upon the forces at my command to give us a direct trail to the dragonriders' home," you say.

The Warrior lifts his head. His eyes grow intense as he awaits your words.

"I can try the Move Time Back spell," you say. "I can try to return us to the moment we defeated Zollah."

"And then?" the Warrior asks, bewildered.

"And then we could climb onto one of the dragons. We could ride the dragon back to their kingdom — ride with the other dragonriders straight to where their real leader resides."

Go on to PAGE 31.

"But you are already weary," the Warrior protests. "Does your magic have the strength?"

"I can only try," you say quietly. You keep your doubts to yourself, as always. You know that this spell is always risky. But you must try it or, you stand little chance of accomplishing your mission.

Can you successfully cast Spell #2 and go back to the time of dragonriders' flight?

Flip a coin twice.

If it comes up the same both times (two heads or two tails), turn to PAGE 6.

If you toss one head and one tail, turn to PAGE 40.

The trail of destruction leads into the forest. The ground is rutted with holes, many of them six feet deep, the holes filled with flattened shrubs, parts of trees that have been knocked down, and the burned corpses of animals who could not get away from the giant dragons in time.

Then suddenly the trail ends.

"This must be magic of some sort," you tell the Wizard. "There is no evidence in the trees that the dragons took flight at this spot."

"Perhaps the dragonriders have called on their own wizards to cast a spell of invisibility over the trail," the Wizard says. "I will try to cast a spell to combat their magic."

You wait for the Wizard to pull his cape around him as he always does to begin his spellcasting. But he does not move. "Are you having trouble with the spell?" you ask.

"Spell?" he says, staring at you. "Would you like me to cast a spell? What sort of spell?"

You stare back at him.

You do not remember what sort of spell. And staring at this strange person in strange clothing, you realize that you do not remember who he is.

Go on to **PAGE 33**.

"Can you help me find my way, stranger?" he asks.

"I am a wayfarer here myself," you answer. "I do not know the way. Can you tell me where we are?"

"I do not remember traveling this way," the stranger replies. "I cannot tell you from where I came. Nor can I recall where I am headed."

You stare at each other, disoriented, frightened. A feeling of dizziness comes over you.

Powerful magic has been used to empty your minds. The trail you wished to follow ends here in the forest. It will never lead you to the dragonriders you wish to defeat.

To accomplish that mission, you will have to face the ancient Jebbarra.

And to do that, you will have to close the book and begin again.

The hideous dragon lowers its head and reaches down to attack.

You know this is your one opportunity.

You grab the beast's neck in your two hands and pull yourself up onto the top of its head. The dragon whips its head back and forth, up and down, trying to throw you off. But you cling to the hot, wet scales and pull yourself up to the back of the head.

Volnar rears up on its hind legs and tosses its head way back. But you cling to its scaly neck. You do not fall off.

You raise your sword in one hand, holding onto the creature's neck with the other hand. You plunge the sword deep into the back of Volnar's neck.

At least, you *try* to plunge the sword into the dragon's neck.

But your sword will not puncture the thick, hot hide.

You have guessed wrong. The back of Volnar's neck is not vulnerable to attack.

The creature snaps its head back and tosses you to the ground. The mouth is open and the head is lowering. The castle grounds ring out with the triumphant cheers of the dragonriders. They are the last sounds you hear — for this adventure has, unhappily, come to an

END

You and your companion walk quickly into the light, eager to see where this pathway leads. The light fills the immense cavern, but the cavern walls still appear to be dark.

What kind of light is this that does not illuminate at all? you ask yourself.

"This is dragonlight," the Wizard says, reading your thoughts. "It is the light that does not light."

You walk farther. The dragonlight dims. You are in darkness again. You continue your journey.

You walk for days. You walk until your hunger, your thirst, your weariness tell you not to walk any farther. But you ignore your defeated bodies. You must continue. You *must*!

Continue walking on PAGE 49.

You and the Wizard enter the second cave slowly, pausing just inside the entrance to allow your eyes to adjust to the dim light. At first, you see nothing in this dark chamber. Then you begin to make out shapes of things — a pile of dried bones in the center of the floor, dozens of fanged bats hanging upside down from the ceiling. . .

"What is that large object on the far wall?" the Wizard asks, his voice echoing off the stone walls of the cave.

You both stare and both realize at the same time that the massive, unmoving object against the wall is none other than Jebbarra!

"Jebbarra, we have found you!" you cry out loudly, attempting to show the ancient dragon that you have no fear.

The dragon does not move. Its wrinkled tail is wrapped tightly around its sagging, yellow body. Cracked, wart-covered eyelids hide its eyes.

"Jebbarra!" you yell again. "Jebbarra, we have come to talk to you!"

One eye opens. The creature is alive. The creature hears you.

Both eyes open. The head swings around slowly on its long, withered neck. Your nostrils fill with the stench of decay.

Go on to PAGE 37.

Jebbarra opens its dry, cracked lips and struggles to speak, but nothing comes out of its mouth but air. "Warrior," the dragon finally manages to say, in a voice that whistles like the wind through a window crack. "Warrior," he repeats, "have you brought this Wizard for my dinner?"

The Wizard takes a step back and looks at you in horror.

"With what teeth could you chew such a morsel?" you ask boldly.

"I would not need to chew a meal so small," Jebbarra wheezes, starts to laugh at his joke, but the laughter turns to violent coughing.

"Go away, Warrior. Let an old dragon sleep," Jebbarra says finally, turning his head away from you.

"Sleep when I am gone," you say, raising your sword. "I need information from you."

The dragon turns to face you once more. "Do you threaten me with that sword?"

"Will you give me cause to use it?" you ask, summoning all your courage before this still-mighty creature.

"You will not leave this cave alive," the dragon says, starting to pull his massive body up, to stand up and face you from his full and awesome height.

Can you talk your way out of this one? Or will you have to fight the old dragon?

Turn to PAGE 52 to find out.

"Who are you?" you cry, assuming a battle stance, the Sword of the Golden Lion cool and light in your hand. "Tell me your name so I will know whom I have defeated!"

"Ha!" cries the armored giant, tossing back his head in a scornful laugh. "Do you think words can shake Wrathgar? Look around you, little Warrior. Do you see the dragons that can be ridden like horses? Do you see this powerful army that travels on dragonback? I, Wrathgar, am responsible for all of it!"

He raises his sword and prepares to strike. "I, Wrathgar, learned the secret of taming these creatures. I, Wrathgar, have built the most powerful army in the world! Do you think I will allow a little wizard and a little warrior to destroy all that I have built here? What impudence!"

You wait for him to begin the fight. But instead of approaching with his sword, Wrathgar gives a loud signal.

Go on to PAGE 39.

The Wizard grabs his cloak and begins one of his spells, but Wrathgar shoves him aside and pins him to the ground. Three flying dragons attack immediately, grinding their hideous, long teeth in anticipation.

The dragons are of three different sizes — small, medium, and big. You have fought such dragon squads in the past. You know that the only way they can be defeated is to kill them in the correct order.

But which is the correct order? Do you start with the smallest dragon and work your way up to the biggest? Or do you try to kill the biggest first, then attack the medium-sized dragon, and finally the smallest dragon?

Your decision will seal your fate.

If you choose to fight the smallest dragon first, turn to **PAGE 45**.

If your choose to start your battle with the biggest dragon, turn to **PAGE 78**.

You draw your cloak tightly around you and begin the incantation for Spell #2, which will move the magical forces to reverse time. You close your eyes as you chant the familiar words.

FLASH!

The spell is done.

But your spell is too powerful. You have moved time back too far. Zollah is still alive. And, the fearful beast advances toward you.

Go on to **PAGE 41**.

Quickly, you decide to try another spell. You decide to attempt Spell #8, The Wind. You will summon a wind, a wind powerful enough to stop this evil foe from advancing. If you succeed, you will have time to try Spell #2 again, Move Time Back, when the dragonriders once again begin their flight.

If you fail, you will have little chance of defeating Zollah and your story will end right here.

Once again you pull your cloak around you and close your eyes. You begin to call out the words that will summon the forces of wind.

Flip a coin.
If it comes up heads, turn to PAGE 10.
If it comes up tails, turn to PAGE 56.

You pull your robes around you and begin to chant the words that will summon the magical forces of the Shift Shape spell. Your wish is to change yourself and the Warrior into dragons. Perhaps the two of you will then be a match for Zollah the Unimaginable.

Will your spell succeed?

Think of a number between one and ten.
If you chose 1, 3, 5, 6, or 7, turn to PAGE 74.
If you chose 2, 4, 8, 9, or 10, turn to PAGE 47.

FLASH!

Clouds fall to earth. Wild animals howl and cry.

Zollah throws you and the Warrior to the ground in fury. "Prepare to die!" the massive creature screams.

Zollah dips his head down low, opens his jaws, revealing jagged and cracked teeth, and dives toward you.

And misses.

Surprised, the dragon attacks again. And misses again.

Your spell has worked! The Mirror Image spell has your foe confused, dizzy.

Zollah pauses for a moment.

"Attack now! *Now!*" you cry to the Warrior.

But the Warrior has missed his opportunity.

Zollah attacks again. But this time the dragon *closes his eyes!*

And you quickly become Zollah's victims.

The Mirror Image spell cannot be effective on one who chooses not to see.

Perhaps you will see a happier ending the next time you venture into the world of *WIZARDS, WARRIORS AND YOU*.

END

Here are the tales Jebbarra tells. One of them tells the truth. It will lead you and the Wizard to the dragonriders you seek. The other is full of lies and will lead you far from your destination.

The First Tale

In the hills of Welknor, where the red rains fall,
the powerful dragons must heed the call
of a magical flute that only they hear —
a music your kingdom will soon learn to fear.

The Second Tale

High on a mountain stands the Castle of Kraal,
defended and hidden by a thousand-foot wall.
Inside, a force of ten thousand men
prepare the dragons to attack once again.

You must decide which tale to believe.

If you choose to travel to the hill of Welknor, turn to **PAGE 80**.

If you choose to travel to the Castle of Kraal, turn to **PAGE 70**.

The dragons fly at you in a straight line. You raise your sword and wait. The flapping of their wings stirs up a wind that thunders about you, the noise becomes a roar as they fly closer, closer, and ...

SLASH!

The smallest dragon makes an easy target. Your sword cuts deep into its belly.

The dragon pulls up in midair, turns, and darts backward. The middle-sized dragon attacks next, digging its teeth deep into your chest. The largest dragon beats the air with its wings, waiting its turn.

You see to your horror that the smallest dragon is preparing another attack. You realize that you have guessed wrong. You have attacked in the wrong order. The small dragon is unharmed.

The dragons have won this battle, and the dragonriders they protect will not be stopped. The secret of the Castle of Kraal will remain a secret, and your mission will go unfinished — until the next time you open this book and attempt to put an end to the siege of the dragonriders.

END

Quickly, as Zollah continues to boast, you wrap your robes around you. You begin to chant the words of the Mirror Image spell, calling up the forces of magic that will reverse your foe's vision.

If you can successfully cast this spell, perhaps — *perhaps* — Zollah will be thrown off balance; perhaps the dragon will be confused enough to throw down its guard. And the Warrior's sword will thrust to victory.

You realize as you use your skills and energies to cast this difficult spell that you stand only a small chance of defeating the mighty Zollah with such trickery.

Will your spell work?

Choose a letter: *A*, *B*, or *C*.
If you choose *A*, turn to PAGE 76.
If you choose *B*, turn to PAGE 94.
If you choose *C*, turn to PAGE 43.

FLASH!

Lightning splits the sky. The ground rumbles and shakes.

Zollah steps back in surprise. He now stares at two exact replicas of himself!

Your spell has worked. You and the Warrior are now twin Zollahs, two powerful dragons to battle together against one.

Cries of confusion and alarm fill the forest clearing. Which is the real Zollah? Which is the leader, and who are the intruders who dare to challenge the mighty Zollah?

You and the Warrior circle your surprised foe slowly. He turns to follow your moves, but he can't keep his eyes on both of you.

The Warrior gives a signal. It is time to attack. Can two new Zollahs defeat the original?

Quick! Turn to PAGE 88 and find out!

FLASH!

The electricity of your magic turns the sky red and melts the clouds. "Has it worked? Have you succeeded?" you hear the Warrior asking. His voice sounds far away.

You fall to your knees, your head pounding, too dizzy to stand. The Warrior takes a few steps forward. "Yes! It's gone!" he calls. "We can proceed."

Because of the energy the difficult Combat Magic spell has used up, you must rest. The next morning, you and your companion set off into the forest. Your horses keep whinnying out warnings of danger.

The danger finds you soon enough. Within a few hours you are seated under a tree, hastily eating a loaf of bread, your only meal of the day. Suddenly, the bushes begin to shake, and loud footsteps crackle on the twig-covered ground.

A dragon, standing upright on two legs, roars an unfriendly greeting and charges toward you. The Warrior tosses aside his bread and unsheathes his sword.

"Wait!" you cry. "Look at how this dragon circles us. Let it capture us. Let it take us prisoner. It will carry us right to the dragonriders!"

"We cannot be sure. I *must* kill it!" the Warrior insists.

You must decide.

Should you try and stop the Warrior from fighting the attacking dragon? If you think so, turn to PAGE 68.

Will it take you to the dragonriders as its prisoners? If you think so, turn to PAGE 11.

The pathway begins to lead downhill and you follow it, breathing heavily, trying ignore the ache in your legs, the growing fear in your heart.

"In ancient scrolls, I have read of endless passageways that wind through eternity," the Wizard says gloomily. "Surely our fortune is not so bad that we have entered upon such a journey."

"Look — a light up ahead!" you cry. You and your companion stagger toward the source of the light.

Have you entered into an endless tunnel? Is it possible that you will wander in this dragon's labyrinth forever?

Turn to PAGE 35.

You and your companion dismount from your faithful horses and approach the fourth cave in the dragon's hill. "There appears to be a doorway of sorts," the Wizard says. "It is likely that Jebbarra has made this protected cave his home."

Slowly, carefully, you reach for the doorway, which is built of a sticky, white substance. Your hand grips the soft edge of the door and prepares to pull it open.

But before you can pull, the doorway bursts forward, pushed by a powerful force — a swarm of gigantic hornets! You have invaded their nest!

Their angry buzz deafens your ears. Two of the giant insects knock over the Wizard and prepare to give him a deadly sting. You reach for the Sword of the Golden Lion, but it is tossed from your hand by the furious swipe of a wing from one of the enraged hornets.

Two of the creatures fly into you at once and send you sprawling to the hard ground. You realize that one sting from one of these monstrous, winged insects will be enough to end your days.

Can you fight them off?

If you have chosen to bring Weapon #2 (the battle-axe), Weapon #5 (the morning star), or Weapon #7 (the flail), turn to PAGE 60.

If you did not choose one of those weapons — OUCH! — that hornet sting has just sent deadly venom coursing through your body. You have only enough time left to realize that this is the end.

"I wish only to speak with you," you call up to Jebbarra. "You must tell us how to find the dragons and the dragonriders who wish to destroy our kingdom!"

The dragon now towers above you, its old head swaying up and down on its long, yellowed neck, its decayed teeth cracked and crumbling in its snarling mouth.

"I do not wish it," Jebbarra says, forcing the words out one at a time. "But I am old and not in the mood to argue. I will tell you what you wish to know —"

"I am grateful —" you start to say.

" — after you entertain me." He calls out a signal. You hear loud scratching sounds. You turn to see two gigantic spiders come scampering into the cave. "Hee, hee, hee," the old dragon starts to laugh, then breaks into another long round of hideous coughing.

"Spiderdragons!" you cry, realizing that these giant spiders have the heads of dragons, and the deadly teeth as well.

"It will take only three bites from my spiderdragons," Jebbarra says, his eyes coming to life for the first time, "and your body will dissolve. Then I will drink you up, and for dessert I'll have your Wizard companion over there. Hee hee."

Go on to PAGE 53.

The spiderdragons' legs scrape and scratch across the cave floor as they race toward you. You raise the Sword of the Golden Lion and begin to swing it in wide circles.

You must kill both spiderdragons. Then, perhaps, Jebbarra will speak to you, and you and the Wizard can flee this cave of horror.

Can you defeat the spiderdragons?

Flip a coin. Each time it comes up *heads*, you have killed a spiderdragon. Each time it comes up *tails*, you have been bitten by a spiderdragon.

To survive, you must get *two* heads before you get *three* tails.

If you manage to get two heads and kill both spiders before you are bitten three times, turn to **PAGE 28**.

If you throw three tails and are bitten three times, you might as well stop reading this. Your body is starting to dissolve, and that hungry look in Jebbarra's eyes gives a pretty good idea of what's going to happen to you next. Jebbarra, and this book, have claimed another victim. The dragonriders still go free — until, perhaps, your next adventure in the world of *WIZARDS, WARRIORS AND YOU*.

The Wizard calls out the words of the ancient spell. He pulls back his robes, and . . . nothing.

The spell has not worked. Your adversary is still huge.

Four dragon heads laugh uproariously. "I was created by a wizard," all four heads say at once. "No wizard's spells can work on me!"

You realize it is time to fight. You draw the Sword of the Golden Lion. One huge dragon head swoops down and grabs it from your hand.

You must try your luck with another one of the weapons you chose to carry on your quest. If you have brought along the battle-axe (Weapon #2), the lance (Weapon #4), or the double-pointed mace (Weapon #8), you have only a one-in-four chance of victory. But even with such poor odds, you must fight. Turn to PAGE 65.

If you have brought along the triple crossbow (Weapon #3) or the longbow with poison-tipped arrows (Weapon #6), you have a slightly better chance of victory. Turn to PAGE 14.

If you have not chosen to bring along any of these weapons, you will soon be joining the hill of bones in the forest clearing. Your legend ends on that hill, and so does this adventure.

The creature's head swoops down low. Volnar attempts to grab you up in its mouth and swallow you whole.

You move quickly — as quickly as you've ever moved. You dart underneath the giant dragon. You pull back your sword and slash with all your might, bringing the blade across the dragon's two front ankles. It has no effect.

Volnar lifts one of his front legs . . .

. . . and steps on you.

The Wizard realizes that you are dead. He pulls his robes around him and attempts to cast a spell to move time backward, to bring you back to life.

But Volnar has him in its mouth before the incantations can be completed. The Wizard has failed, too.

This story has become the story of the triumph of Volnar the Invulnerable. It is a story you probably do not wish to continue. It is a story you are pleased to see has come to the word . . .

END

FLASH!

The wind whistles at first. Then the whistle becomes a howl, the howl a deafening roar.

"You've done it!" cries the Warrior joyfully as Zollah is swooped up in a giant twisting cone of wind.

But his joy is premature.

"The wind!" you cry in horror. "It — it's out of control!"

The wind turns back upon you and the Warrior. The full force of your spell has been turned on you. You feel yourself being lifted off the ground by the wind. You see your companion struggling to stay on his feet. But within seconds, you and the Warrior are lifted up over the trees, over the army of dragonriders, away, away over the forest — the wind carrying you toward the

END

You begin to run toward the rampaging dragons even before you have completed the final words of your spell.

Will the momentary darkness you create give you time to sneak up on this destructive foe?

FLASH!

Darkness.

It lasts only a second.

You and your companion are standing in the open field. Your spell was *not* effective.

But there will soon be another darkness for you. Sadly, it won't be momentary.

The dragonriders see that you and the Warrior are easy prey.

The only magical act that can save you now is to close your book — and to disappear from the world of *WIZARDS, WARRIORS AND YOU!*

END

The dragons rumble through the forest, trampling trees and bushes as they walk. Soon a command is given. The creatures raise giant wings and take to the air.

You and the Warrior grasp the hot, scaly neck of the dragon you are riding and stare in amazement at the earth far below.

Forest gives way to barren plains. A river cuts through red rock. Solid sheets of rock build up to a snowcapped mountain. And still the dragons fly.

Your destination comes into view many hours later. It is a large, black castle built on a jutting cliff on a mountain of black rock. The dragons descend into a rock courtyard where long troughs holding food and water await them. Their riders dismount and walk toward a low, stone barracks at the far end of the castle courtyard.

"What strange castle is this, built of rock upon rock?" the Warrior asks.

Your heart is pounding. Your mind is filled with all kinds of images. "I know this castle," you say quietly.

Go on to PAGE 59.

"You have been here on this black mountain before?" the Warrior asks, surprised.

"It is the castle of the wizard named Warrick," you tell your partner. "A wizard of the dark forces. This black castle suits him well."

"And how do you come to know him?" the Warrior asks.

Your voice trembles as you struggle to answer. "He is my brother," you say.

The Warrior stares at you in disbelief. "Did I hear you correctly?"

"Yes," you say sadly. "It appears that to accomplish our mission, I must destroy my own brother!"

This may be the most difficult challenge you have ever faced. Can you use your powers against your own brother?

Turn to PAGE 92.

The hornets, as big as vultures, swarm around you and your companion. You feel the warmth of their hairy bodies, the tangy odor of their breath as they buzz by your head preparing to sting.

If you have brought the battle-axe, the morning star, or the flail, you may still have a chance to fight for your life against the attacking hornets. To survive, you must kill three hornets. If you do so, the others will retreat into their nest.

Toss a coin five times. Each time it comes up tails, you have killed a hornet. If it comes up at least three times out of the five tosses, you have killed three hornets. You have survived! Turn to PAGE 67.

If you do *not* come up with three tails, the hornets have beaten you. In fact, you might say you have suffered a stinging defeat!

Your mission ends here at the mouth of this cave, far from the dragonriders you wish to defeat. Better luck next time you travel the dangerous paths in the world of *WIZARDS, WARRIORS AND YOU*.

"*Halt!* Who goes there? What evil sorcery has been committed here?" cries a loud, angry voice.

The voice seems to waken everyone — and every dragon — from the spell. The castle grounds fill with movement and noise, the cries of men discovering the two intruders in their midst and the low growls of awakening dragons.

A giant of a man — eight feet tall at least — wearing the armor of a knight, comes running toward you, sword in hand.

You grab your sword and prepare to do battle.

Your battle begins on PAGE 38.

The spells you have decided to use against your brother, the wizard Warrick, are called Power Spells. They are so potent and are used so rarely, they do not even appear in *The Book of Spells*.

Power Spells are used to drain the power from another wizard. You decide to use five Power Spells against Warrick. Each one will drain some of his magical abilities from him.

If Warrick matches your spells, the effect will be reversed, and *you* will be the one who loses power.

For each of the five Power Spells, flip two coins. The first coin is yours. The second coin is Warrick's. If your toss comes up heads, Warrick's toss must also come up heads in order for him to match your magic.

If Warrick's coin *fails* to match your coin, you have successfully cast a Power Spell upon him. Each time Warrick's coin *does* match your coin, he has drained power from *you*.

Cast five spells, tossing both coins five times. If Warrick *fails* to match your coin at least three times out of the five tosses, turn to PAGE 24.

If Warrick *does* match your coin at least three times out of the five tosses, turn to PAGE 84.

You realize you must act fast, for once Zollah has tired of boasting about how he has enslaved humans to fight for dragons, he will kill you instantly.

You think of three spells that might help you defeat this mighty foe and free the soldiers from the spell that enslaves them.

Spell #1 (Shift Shape): You could change yourself and the Warrior into dragons and battle it out with Zollah.

Spell #6 (Mirror Image): You could cause Zollah to see everything in reverse. This would confuse him so that the Warrior might be able to defeat him in a battle.

Spell #11 (Shrink): You could attempt to reduce Zollah to the size of a mouse. If this spell works, he could be easily defeated.

Quickly make your choice.
If you choose to try Spell #1, turn to PAGE 42.
If you choose to try Spell #6, turn to PAGE 46.
If you choose to try Spell #11, turn to PAGE 82.

You pull your cloak around you and begin to chant the words of the spell. But before you complete the spell, you hear an eerie silence.

The wind has stopped.

Zollah is no longer held back by its force.

The silence is broken by the sound of attacking dragons. The next sound you hear will be screaming — yours!

To avoid this hideous sound, close the book quickly. This attempt to defeat the dragonriders has come to an unpleasant and noisy

END

The four heads swoop down quickly, ready to enjoy their dinner. The Wizard drops back, still horrified that his spell has not worked against this hideous dragon.

You prepare to use either your battle-axe, your lance, or your double-pointed mace against this large and menacing foe. You know your chances are not very good, for you must kill all four bodies before one of them eats you.

Toss a coin four times. If it comes up heads *only once* in the four tosses, you can defeat the Dragon of Four Bodies! Turn to PAGE 85.

If the coin comes up heads more than once in four tosses, none of your weapons have saved you. The dragon has claimed two more victims, adding a Wizard and a Warrior to its hill of bones, ending your adventure in this dreary, empty forest clearing.

"You have defeated the Dragon of Four Bodies," the Wizard says quietly, still staring at the fallen creature. "But your victory brings us no closer to the dragonriders. We have allowed Jebbarra to fool us. We have followed the wrong path by choosing to believe the wrong tale. Now here we sit in this empty clearing, far from where our mission should lead us."

"We still have horses to carry us where we will," you protest. "And we still have the strength to —"

But your words are cut short by a voice that booms through the clearing, an angry voice that shakes the trees:

"WHAT HAVE YOU DONE TO MY CHILD?!"

Another dragon steps out from the trees. Another Dragon of Four Bodies. The four bodies are so tall, the heads must duck under the clouds to see down to the ground.

"WHAT HAVE YOU DONE TO MY CHILD?!" the four giant heads cry in grief and in fury.

And you realize that no answer you can give will help keep you alive in this unfortunate confrontation with an angry parent!

END

You kill the last hornet and toss its bloodied carcass down the hill. The Wizard is at your side now as the rest of the giant hornets retreat far into their cave.

You and your companion are both shaken, exhausted from your battle against these monstrous insects. "Perhaps Jebbarra has defeated us this time," you suggest to the Wizard. "I do not believe we are strong enough to face that ancient dragon in his own home now."

The Wizard agrees. "There are other paths that lead to the dragonriders who destroyed our crops and threaten our freedom," he says. "Let us return to the castle and follow the path the dragonriders have left in our forest."

You agree. Jebbarra could defeat you easily in your worn condition. The trip back will give you time to steady your mind and refresh your aching muscles.

Then you will follow the path of destruction left by the evil dragonriders.

You can begin to follow that path by turning to **PAGE 32**.

You try to stop the Warrior from attacking the dragon, but still he leaps at the beast, thrusting his sword forward. The dragon jumps to the left and swings its long, heavy tail, knocking the Warrior over and pinning your partner to the ground.

The dragon picks you up off the ground with its teeth and tosses you onto its hot, scaly back. After an instant, the Warrior is beside you on the dragon's back, and the dragon has left the ground, making its way through the tangled trees to open sky.

Your eyes open wide in amazement as you look at the world below. The trip, however, is a short one. In a clearing that rapidly comes into view stand the hundreds of dragons and their riders.

The dragon has carried you to the destination you sought. But what fate awaits you there?

Turn to PAGE 22.

You ride your horses at full gallop, for the journey to the Castle of Kraal is a long one, and you have already wasted too much time.

"Jebbarra is not as wise as he thinks," you tell the Wizard. "It was easy for a person who has traveled this land to know that his tale of Welknor contained falsehoods. For there are no hills in Welknor. And the rains that fall over that distant land are violet, not red."

"Jebbarra has not left his cave in many decades," the Wizard says, ducking under a low tree limb that seems to fly overhead as your horses pound the soft earth of the forest. "Perhaps his memory is failing him. Ha ha!"

Go on to PAGE 71.

A few days later, weary from your fast journey, the two of you stand on a grassy hill. The Castle of Kraal stands before you in its orange splendor. And even from a distance you can see the many guards that patrol its towers.

"They have a secret to hide, that is certain," you say, shielding your eyes from the sun so you may view the guards in the towers. "I would venture to say that the dragons and their riders are behind that well-guarded fortress. Now, how shall we gain entrance?"

"Let us go closer to the wall that surrounds the castle," the Wizard suggests. "If we can get close enough without being detected, I can cast a spell to put the guards to sleep. I cannot predict how long the spell will last, but it will be long enough at least for us to gain entrance to the castle grounds and see if this is indeed the dragons' lair we seek."

You agree that this is a good plan.

Slowly, you ride down the hill. You keep to the shadows to keep from being seen. A cloud rolls over the sun, casting the entire ground in shadow, helping you to get close enough for the Wizard to perform the sleep spell.

Soon you are near the castle wall, still undetected. The Wizard pulls his robes around him and begins to chant the words of the ancient spell.

Will he be able to put all of the guards to sleep?

Turn to **PAGE 90** to find out.

Volnar utters a deafening cry and rushes forward to attack. He ducks his jagged teeth down, throws open his massive jaw, and prepares to finish you off in one bite.

But you leap away from his gaping mouth and run at full speed toward his tail. The giant creature turns to follow you, lifts its head once again, and prepares another attack.

You raise the Sword of the Golden Lion and, as the hideous creature bends down to grab you in its teeth, you drive your blade deep into its tail. Again. Again.

Volnar howls in pain, its giant head rearing up into the air, its bright brown tongue falling out one side of its mouth. Your sword has chopped off the dragon's tail. Its eyes open wide in horror. It falls over backwards, hitting the ground with an ear-shattering crash.

You have found Volnar's vulnerable spot. The dragon cannot get up. It will never stand again.

The castle courtyard fills with cries of horror as everyone witnesses your victory over this mighty foe. You raise your sword and turn to face Wrathgar. But he is running away, running as fast as he can from the castle grounds toward the forest.

You soon realize why. The dragons below you in the courtyard have reared up in anger and are turning against the men who rode them.

Go on to **PAGE 73.**

It was Volnar, not Wrathgar, who ruled this place, you now realize. As long as Volnar reigned, the dragons allowed themselves to be mastered by Wrathgar and his riders. But with their leader unable to stand over them, the dragons no longer had to obey. Wrathgar fled because he knew the dragons would now turn on their former masters and murder them all.

"Let us leave this place. Our task is accomplished," you call to the Wizard, shouting over the cries and chaos in the courtyard. "There are horses by the wall. We will borrow them for our journey. I don't believe there will be any men to ride them."

Turn to PAGE 83 and enjoy your journey home.

FLASH!

The sky seems to tremble and birds cry out.

Your spell has worked.

Or has it?

You look over to the Warrior and your eyes fill with horror.

Zollah's magic has proven more powerful than yours. Zollah's magic has twisted yours, confused it, turned it back on itself.

You have changed shape, it is true. You are now the Warrior. The Warrior is now you.

The two of you do not have time to enjoy your new identities. The last sounds you hear are the roars of laughter of Zollah and his army. And now, the powerful dragon is moving in for the kill.

Your magic has failed you this time.

But perhaps there will be other times. And perhaps Zollah will not have the last laugh.

END

FLASH!

Birds cry out and the trees bend low to the ground.

You look up. Zollah is not to be seen.

You look down — and there the dragon stands. Your spell has worked. Zollah is a tiny creature, no more than two inches tall.

Smiling for the first time in a long while, you reach down and grab for the tiny dragon. You miss. Little Zollah darts between your legs.

You and the Warrior both try to stamp on it. But you are not quick enough.

The tiny Zollah runs into the crowd of dragon onlookers. You try desperately to find him. You know your spell cannot last long. You must find Zollah and destroy him before the spell wears off and he returns to his normal —

Too late!

The mighty dragon reappears — as tall and menacing as ever — in the midst of his fellow dragons. The ground shakes as he shoves dragons out of his way in his fury to get to you.

Your magic has failed you and, sadly, you have failed King Henry. Close the book now. You know well that in the world of *WIZARDS, WARRIORS AND YOU*, success may be just a few pages away!

END

FLASH!

Distant trees fall and birds shriek in their nests.

Zollah drops you and the Warrior to the ground and takes a step back, the ground shaking beneath his heavy footstep.

"What have you done, Wizard?" he cries. "Do not bother to answer. Your time has ended, anyway. Prepare to die!"

Zollah dips his giant head down. Hot drool pours from his open mouth as he prepares to swallow you whole.

Has the Mirror Image spell worked?

The giant jaws snap at air.

Zollah has missed. Confused, he turns his attention to the Warrior.

But his eyes do not look at the Warrior. Once again the powerful jaws snap, enclosing nothing but air.

Zollah roars in fury and stamps the ground.

"I will crush you both!" the dragon screams.

But his feet do not even come close as they pound the forest floor, leaving large holes of barren dirt where grass once stood.

Zollah's talons slash out in all directions. But once again his attack is misdirected. Each failed attempt to destroy you makes the powerful dragon more angry. And as his fury grows, his attacks become wilder and wilder.

Go on to PAGE 77.

"AAAAAIIIIII!" Zollah screams out his displeasure, his fury, his confusion, as his slaves and fellow dragons look on in terror and disbelief.

The dragon is in a frenzy now, pawing the ground, slashing out with its claws, stamping and screaming, snapping his awesome jaws.

The Warrior unsheathes the Sword of the Golden Lion now. He steps forward carefully, deliberately — and slices off Zollah's head.

THUD. The heavy head hits the ground.

The massive body falls. You are victorious. But you have no time to enjoy your victory. Before Zollah has let out his final death sigh, the dragonriders have mounted their dragons and the dragons have taken to the air. The flap of their wings as the giant bodies soar aloft is deafening, and you shield your eyes from the wind.

"They fly to the South!" the Warrior cries.

"Zollah lied to us," you realize "There is someone even more powerful than he who leads these dragonriders! If Zollah were their master they would not flee. We must continue on our mission," you say, unable to hide the weariness from your voice. "But now there is no easy path to follow, no one to lead us to our foe."

How will you find the real leader of the dragonriders?

Turn to **PAGE 30**.

SLASH!

Your sword cuts deep into the belly of the biggest dragon. It shrieks, raising its head in anger and pain.

The second dragon flies to the attack, but your sword is ready.

Suddenly you are surrounded by the beating wings of these ferocious adversaries. You swing your sword furiously. You cannot tell which dragon you are fighting as you dodge and duck away from their snarling mouths and outstretched claws.

SLASH. SLASH!

The fight seems to last for hours. At last, the dragons are slowing down. At last, the dragons are weakening. Your arm is growing heavy. It takes inhuman effort to swing your sword. When you think you can swing the sword no longer, the last dragon — the smallest one — falls.

You have chosen the correct order in which to defeat the flying dragons, and you have defeated them.

You drop to one knee, exhausted, your entire body aching from your efforts. You look up — and realize that your battle has just begun!

Turn to PAGE 86.

The journey to Welknor is long and hard. Your weary horses make their way through tangled forests without paths and over a rock-strewn plain that cuts their hooves and bruises their legs. The journey ends in another forest.

"Jebbarra's tale told of hills, but this land is flat," the Wizard says to you.

"What is that hill up ahead?" you cry, seeing something strange in a small clearing. Your horses carry you close enough to see what it is. "It *is* a hill, all right! A hill of bones!" you cry.

"Perhaps it is some sort of burial hill," the Wizard suggests, climbing down from his horse to take a closer look.

"No — it is our dining room!" shouts a thunderous voice from the trees beyond the clearing. "Welcome, dinner!"

An orange dragon rumbles out from behind a tree, a hideous grin across its drooling mouth. Another dragon steps out, another follows, and then another. But soon you realize that you are seeing not four dragons — but one! They are all attached at the tail. "The Dragon of Four Bodies!" you cry, recognizing this legendary beast.

Go on to PAGE 81.

The dragon uses its four bodies to form a wall around you and the Wizard. "Jebbarra has sent me a tasty lunch this time!" the dragon says, its drool running down all four of its hungry mouths.

You are surrounded by the flesh of the dragon's four bodies. Four hungry heads close in on you.

"I will attempt a spell," the Wizard cries, pulling his robes around him. "I will shrink the dragon down until it is the size of a dog. Then we can make our escape!"

He begins to chant the words of the ancient spell. Will it work?

Turn to PAGE 54 to find out.

You grab your robes and pull them around you to begin casting the Shrink spell. If only the dragon doesn't notice, if only you have enough time . . .

If you can shrink Zollah down small enough, he can be stamped out, the way he plans to stamp you out. But this is a complicated spell to cast, and you know you don't have much time.

Can you summon the forces of magic to shrink the powerful dragon — before Zollah realizes what you are doing?

To find out, close your eyes and see which color you visualize first: red, yellow, blue, or green. As soon as you have seen — or imagined — one of these colors stronger than the others, open your eyes.

If you saw red or green, turn to PAGE 95.

If you saw blue or yellow, turn to PAGE 75.

A few moments later, you and your partner are riding through the forest, quietly savoring your victory. "We will be home before the harvest is ended," the Wizard says. "And now we can know for certain that there will be food for all this winter."

"But will we be home this winter to enjoy it?" you ask. "By now, King Henry probably has a new mission for us that will take us to places we have not yet imagined." You ride in silence for a few moments. Then you add with a grin, "I'd be very disappointed if he doesn't!"

You and the Wizard enjoy a good laugh. You both know that home is not a place to stay — it is a place to begin an adventure.

END

If you would like to play the role of the Wizard when you set out on your next adventure, turn to PAGE 15.

You fall to the ground.

"What is happening?" cries the Warrior.

You feel too weak to answer.

"I am so . . . so . . ."

Warrick tosses back his head in another long and loud laugh. "I have matched your magic, brother!" he calls down. "You are the Wizard no longer. But have no fear. I have employment for you. And for your friend."

You struggle to stand. You and the Warrior are surrounded by dragonriders. "Take them to the stable boys' quarters!" Warrick bellows. "We will begin to teach them all there is to know about the care and cleaning of dragons tomorrow — early tomorrow morning!"

You hear his laughter as you and your partner are dragged away. Even in your weakened state, you realize that you have failed.

You had better close the book now — unless you wish to learn about the care and feeding of dragons. That, it appears, is how you will be spending your days from now on, until you come to the

END

You chose the right weapon, and you wielded it skillfully. The four bodies of the dreadful dragon lie still.

"Jebbarra's tale sent us down the wrong path," you say to the Wizard, watching the horizon for the approach of other foes. "The only hill of Welknor is that hill of bones. Jebbarra sent us into this trap, but my weapons proved more powerful than his hungry dragon brother."

"His other tale — how skillfully he told it to make us believe it was not the true one!" the Wizard says. "It told of the Castle of Kraal, which is far from here."

"But that castle must now be our destination."

"Yes, that is where we will find our foes," you tell him somberly, "and that is where we shall defeat them."

What dangers await you in the Castle of Kraal?

Turn to PAGE 71.

"Ha ha! Very impressive!" Wrathgar yells. "But that was a small victory, Warrior! My dragons and army will not fall to our knees and beg you for mercy because you survived the attack of three flying dragons!"

"Your hours are numbered, Wrathgar!" you shout, pulling yourself up, preparing for your next fight. "Your dragonriders will not terrorize the people of this kingdom any longer!"

Wrathgar laughs at your boast. He gives another loud signal. All eyes turn toward the far wall. "Poor Warrior," Wrathgar calls, turning down the corners of his mouth in mock sorrow, "you are about to face Volnar the Invulnerable!"

You have heard tales of Volnar the Invulnerable. Has Wrathgar somehow managed to tame this legendary dragon, too?

The ground rumbles, the stones of the castle shake. The entire courtyard shakes. Volnar the Invulnerable enters. Red eyes burn into yours; smoking nostrils inhale, sniff your presence. The immense creature is taking a few seconds to size you up.

You remember the legend of Volnar. The dragon is invulnerable — it cannot be killed, except in one spot on its body. Only that one spot can be successfully attacked.

But where? *Where?* If only you could remember . . .

Go on to PAGE 87.

The creature lifts its ugly head and snarls, its jagged green teeth bared, its red eyes never leaving yours.

Your mind races desperately. You are thinking ... thinking ... trying to remember the one vulnerable spot on this dreaded foe, trying to remember before the inevitable attack.

Is it the back of the neck that is vulnerable to attack?

Is it the creature's ankles?

Or is it the darting, throbbing tail?

You can't remember. You just can't remember. You're going to have to guess — and hope you've guessed correctly!

The dragon — its eyes piercing into yours, smoke pouring from its mouth and dripping nostrils — walks slowly toward you.

The time has come. You must decide which part of Volnar to attack with your sword.

If you choose to attack the back of the neck, turn to PAGE 34.

If you think you should attack the ankles, turn to PAGE 55.

If you think you should attack the tail, turn to PAGE 72.

"AAAAAARGH!"

You raise your head and roar to the skies. You and the Warrior push your gigantic dragon bodies forward, bare your jagged teeth, rise up to attack.

"AAAAARGH!"

This time it is Zollah who screams.

Your teeth sink deep into dragonflesh. The Warrior uses his powerful forearms to slash and tear.

Zollah falls, and still you continue the attack.

Zollah weakens. Zollah closes his eyes. Zollah dies.

You and the Warrior — victorious Zollahs — stand over the once-mighty leader. You turn to the audience of startled dragons and soldiers.

But the soldiers and dragons ignore your victory. The soldiers leap onto the dragons' backs, and in seconds the dragons are up in the air, flying at full speed toward the south.

The spell that turned you to dragons wears off. Your old faces return, faces filled with surprise. "Zollah must not be the leader of these dragonriders after all," you say. "If they were under his power, they would not have fled. The dragonriders must be going to their true leader."

"How will we ever find them now?" asks the Warrior. "They're all gone."

Turn to PAGE 30.

FLASH!

The cloud over the sun crumbles and falls from the sky. A blinding light turns blue, then bright red. When all returns to normal, you look up to the towers. The guards are slumped against the stones, asleep where they stood. The spell has worked.

"Remember," warns the Wizard as the two of you ride right up to the wall, "this spell is unpredictable. It may last for hours — or for minutes."

You throw a looped rope up to the top of the wall, and it catches on a stone. Then you both pull yourselves up to the top of the wall.

You look down, and your mouths actually drop open in amazement!

Before you stands an unbelievable sight — the entire castle grounds filled with dragons of all descriptions and sizes, dragons and their riders, dragons and their trainers, dragons of myth and legend — now as tame as horses or dogs.

The dragons all sleep where they stand, as do the men who train and ride them. The Wizard's spell has worked well. Or has it?

Someone approaches!

Turn to PAGE 61.

FLASH!

The sky blackens and the earth along with it. All is dark.

Your spell has worked, but there is no time to congratulate yourself. You and the Warrior run as fast as you can — taking giant, leaping steps — until you are next to the dragons and their mystified riders.

As the sky brightens again and the Momentary Darkness spell wears off, you pull yourselves up onto the back of a dragon. The dragonriders are still baffled by the sudden darkness. One swing of the Warrior's sword is all it takes to defeat the rider of this dragon. The Warrior gives him a shove, and he topples off the creature's shoulders. You and the Warrior take his place unnoticed.

The dragonriders turn their beasts and rise into the air. They do not realize that two new riders have joined their flight to their leader.

Your plan is working. So far.

Where will the dragon carry you?

Turn to PAGE 58.

A few moments later, Warrick steps out onto a balcony to greet his returning troops. "Why, brother!" he cries, spotting you immediately down below him in the courtyard. (Did he know all along that you were coming? You would not put that beyond his powers.) "I am honored that you have decided to pay a visit of kinship," he calls down.

"I have not come in brotherly love," you call up to him. "Your army has destroyed the crops that were to feed my kingdom this winter."

"*Your* kingdom?" Warrick calls out, throwing back his head and enjoying a hearty laugh. "Brother, all kingdoms are mine now! By casting a spell on these dragons, I have built a fighting force that will hold all kingdoms under my control!"

Go on to Page 93.

You look up at your brother. Your mind is flooded with memories, memories of your childhood, happy memories of the two of you learning magic together from the old wizard who taught you.

"You *can* be stopped!" you call up, pushing the memories from your mind. "I have come to stop you. I have no choice but to fight for the freedom of my kingdom, to carry out the mission assigned me by King Henry."

"*I* am the only king now!" your brother bellows, his smile gone now, his face filled with dark fury.

The dragons look up from their food troughs, annoyed by the argument. The dragonriders have filled the courtyard, their weapons in their hands. They stand silently, confused by the battling words of their leader and the bold intruder. The Warrior stands besides you, a hand on the hilt of his sword.

"Make a move!" your brother calls down, taunting you. "Try what you will! My magic will match your magic! I have the power to control dragons. I can surely control *you*!"

"You must accept his challenge," the Warrior says.

"Yes," you say softly. "His magic may be more than the equal of mine. But I have no choice but to accept his challenge. I will not waste time with minor spells. As much as I regret the need for it, I will call up the most powerful magic at my command. I will summon spells I have never dared try before."

Will these special spells be powerful enough to defeat your brother?

Turn to **PAGE 62**.

FLASH!

The clouds turn red and the wind stops.

"What are you attempting, Wizard?" Zollah cries, dropping you and the Warrior to the ground.

The dragon takes a step back. And then another.

Has your spell worked? Is the mighty dragon in a state of confusion? Is that why Zollah continues to back up?

"Charge him! Charge him *now*!" you call to the Warrior.

He unsheathes his sword and rushes forward. But he misses the dragon completely. The Warrior thrusts forward again with his sword. But he is not even close to his foe now.

Zollah rears back its massive head and fills the sky with laughter.

You realize what has happened. The dragon has turned your magic back on you and your partner. *Your* vision has been reversed.

Your luck has run out in this forest clearing.

Actually, you do have just a tiny bit of luck left. Since your vision has been reversed, you do not see Zollah as he moves forward to attack you.

This last little bit of luck will have to last you — sad to say — until your next attempt to defeat the dragonriders.

END

FLASH!

The ground turns red, then pales to white. The sun blackens and the air turns cold.

Your spell has worked!

Zollah stands before you — only three inches tall!

Sadly, however, you cannot rejoice in your success. In your haste to cast the spell, you made a few major miscalculations.

You shrank Zollah down to three inches. But you also shrank yourself and the Warrior. The two of you now stand *one* inch tall! Zollah is still a giant to you!

You have a *small* amount of time left — just enough to close this book and hope for *bigger* success in your next adventure!

END

The Book of Spells

For use only by the WIZARD

As the Wizard, you may use any of these powerful spells. But remember, magic is mysterious and unpredictable. Use it wisely.

Spell #1: Shift Shape

This spell allows you to change shape, to assume the appearance of an animal, plant, or any object as long as it is *within view*. The spell can also be used to change the appearance of others. You cannot use this spell to change into the shape of something that is not within open view. The spell lasts for only a few minutes. It wears off suddenly, returning the subject to his or her former appearance.

Spell #2: Move Time Back

This spell allows you to move time backward. The spell can move time back one hour at the most. You can then change events by acting in a different manner during that hour. The drawback of this spell is that it's impossible to predict the precise amount of time that will be reversed—it can be anywhere from five minutes up to an hour.

Spell #3: Momentary Darkness

A sudden darkness that lasts up to five seconds is conjured up by this spell. The spell is most useful for taking someone by surprise. The darkness is total—but you must move quickly, since the darkness lasts such a short time.

Spell #4: Invisibility

A basic spell known even by apprentice sorcerers, you can use the Invisibility spell to become instantly and completely invisible.

A useful spell for fast escapes from desperate situations, it has one major drawback—the length of time the invisibility lasts cannot be predicted. It can last for as long as several weeks, or for as brief a period as a few seconds.

This spell can also be used to make an enemy or an ally invisible.

Spell #5: Invisible Shield

An invisible shield can be conjured up that completely encircles you and your companions. The shield cannot be penetrated by any weapon, although fire can be used to destroy it. The shield lasts as long as the spellcaster wishes it to. But a major drawback to this spell is that the shield is immovable. If the user moves more than a few feet in any direction, the shield disappears.

Spell #6: Mirror Image

When this spell is cast upon a foe, it causes the foe to see everything in reverse as if he or she were looking into a mirror. Especially effective for duels, this spell is used to confuse one's enemies and throw them off balance. It lasts for about five minutes.

Spell #7: Sorcerer's Sleep

This spell can be used to put anyone standing within 100 feet of you to sleep immediately. The spell can work on one person or on 500 people at once. The major drawback to this spell is that the length of time the foe will sleep cannot be predicted. It may be just for a few seconds, or a few days.

Spell #8: The Wind

This spell conjures up a hurricane force wind, strong enough to blow away the toughest foe. A most dangerous spell, it must be used with the utmost care—for once the wind has been summoned, it cannot be controlled. It may turn against the spellcaster as easily as against the persons it is intended to defeat.

Spell #9: Merlin's Fire

This spell can be used to start a blazing fire on any object. It cannot be used on people or animals. The fire burns with intensity and cannot be extinguished until the spell is removed. This is a dangerous spell because the fire can spread out of control within seconds if the wind should change directions.

(*Note*: This spell is named for Merlin but there is no known account of his having used it.)

Spell #10: Visions

This spell will cause a foe to start seeing things, all kinds of things that exist only in his or her mind! An incapacitating spell, it will cause the foe to lose all sight of what is real and what is not. Advanced wizards can even control what visions a foe will see. A difficult spell to cast, because it sometimes backfires and affects the spellcaster rather than the enemy.

Spell #11: Shrink

This spell causes a foe or foes to shrink in size. Its effect is immediate and can be used on anyone—or anything—within 100 yards. As with other spells, it is impossible to predict exactly how small someone will become or how long he or she will stay that way.

Spell #12: Combat Magic

This spell allows you to combat a magic spell that has been used against you or against a companion. It will immediately dispel any magic, except that of a Grand Wizard. This spell requires such concentration and energy that after performing it the spellcaster must rest for one entire day. *The spell can be used only once during an adventure.*

Now that you have studied your spells, you may begin your adventure on PAGE 20.

The Book of Weapons

For use only by
the WARRIOR

**As the Warrior, you may use all the
weapons listed here. But remember,
a great warrior uses wisdom
as well as might.**

Weapon #1: The Sword of the Golden Lion

An immortal sword that cannot be broken, the Sword of the Golden Lion was forged by the same swordsmith who forged the legendary Excalibur. The scabbard carries the inscription *Forever*, and a lion is etched in gold on the blade itself. You won the sword after a battle to the death against the Lancashire Sorcerer, and it has been at your side ever since.

YOU CARRY THE SWORD OF THE GOLDEN LION AT ALL TIMES. IN ADDITION, YOU MAY CHOOSE FROM THE FOLLOWING LIST THREE OTHER WEAPONS TO ACCOMPANY YOU.

Weapon #2: Battle-Axe

A favorite weapon of King Henry himself, the battle-axe can be useful when there is little room to wield a sword. With a head that weighs 20 pounds, the weight and the sharpness of its cutting edge make it a valued weapon for the knight who's strong enough to use it.

Weapon #3: Triple Crossbow

Designed especially for you by the Wizard, this crossbow has a span of three feet. It can propel three arrows at once in three different directions. This makes it especially useful in those situations when the Warrior fights alone against many.

Weapon #4: Lance

The eight-foot-long lance is an excellent weapon for battles on horseback. It is usually the weapon knights turn to when their sword has failed them. The major drawback to the lance is the fact that it can be broken.

Weapon #5: Morning Star

This weapon is guaranteed to leave its mark on a victim's memory. Sharp spikes jut out of a wooden ball, which is attached by a chain to a long wooden handle. The weapon isn't effective against armor, but is an excellent choice for inflicting head wounds.

Weapon #6: Longbow with Poison-tipped Arrows

A simple weapon, except that the poison tips were prepared especially by the Wizard. Their potency never weakens, no matter how many victims the arrows claim.

Weapon #7: Flail

Used for whipping or choking, this is largely a weapon for desperate situations. It consists of a short wooden stick attached by a long cord to a long wooden handle. Major benefit of this weapon is that it is light and easier to carry than most weapons.

Weapon #8: Double-pointed Mace

A long mace with two deadly sharp points on the head, this weapon can be slung by a loop on the wrist and used as a club, as a spear, or as a deadly lance. Many have wondered about the history of this—the only double-pointed mace in the kingdom. But you have refused to reveal its origin.

Weapon #9: Devil's Dagger

This dagger resembles a small sword except that the blade is shorter and thinner. The dagger is worn on the side opposite the sword and is usually used to deliver a death blow to someone who has already fallen. Your dagger is called the Devil's Dagger because of your superhuman skill at using it.

Now that you are suitably armed for your quest, you may begin the adventure on PAGE 8.

About the Author

Eric Affabee has been a journalist, a fisherman, and a professional soldier. He currently lives in Cleveland, Ohio, with his many pets. This is his first published book.

About the Illustrator

Earl Norem has been a successful illustrator for many years. His work has appeared in Marvel Comics and Magazines, *Reader's Digest*, and many other publications. Earl and his family live in New Milford, Connecticut.

WIZARDS, WARRIORS & YOU™

A new series of fantasy role-playing adventures of skill, daring and danger!

• • •

In each WIZARDS, WARRIORS & YOU™ adventure
the reader chooses the role of either the Wizard or
the Warrior before embarking on a perilous quest
through a mythical kingdom ruled by monsters and dragons.
As the Wizard, the reader takes the Book of Spells
and is master of all its mysterious, magical powers.
As the Warrior, the reader uses the Book of Weapons,
a complete arsenal of deadly arms,
to prevail against all challengers.

Each book includes dozens of adventures, and can be
played over and over again in each role,
with a different outcome every time.

• • •

#1 THE FOREST OF TWISTED DREAMS
　　R.L. Stine　　　　　　　　　　　　88047-4/$2.50

#2 THE SIEGE OF THE DRAGONRIDERS
　　Eric Affabee　　　　　　　　　　　88054-4/$2.50

Coming in November

#3 WHO KIDNAPPED PRINCESS SARALINDA?
　　Megan Stine & H. William Stine　　89268-5/$2.50

#4 GHOST KNIGHTS OF CAMELOT
　　David Anthony Kraft　　　　　　　89276-6/$2.50

More to come! Ask for them in your bookstore.

AVON Paperbacks